ONE HORSE

FARM by Dahlov Ipcar

DOUBLEDAY & COMPANY, INC., GARDEN CITY, NEW YORK

LITHOGRAPHED IN THE U.S.A.

Big Betty was the one horse on a one horse farm. She was big and strong with big clumping feet.

Betty had not always been big and strong.

Once she had been a little baby colt with long wobbly legs. She was born in the big barn early one morning.

She was born the same day as the farmer's son Johnny.

Betty grew fast and Johnny grew slow. When Johnny was five years old Big Betty was all grown up as big as she ever would be and working hard on his father's farm. Johnny loved Big Betty. He loved to watch her working.

Betty liked to work and there was lots of work for her to do. It was Betty who pulled the plow that plowed the big fields, turning over long furrows with the old grass underneath and the brown dirt on top.

It was Betty who pulled the disk harrow that smoothed the rough furrows the plow had made.

It was Betty who pulled the seeder that planted the seeds in the fields. The corn seeds and the vegetable seeds and the new grass seeds.

It was Betty who pulled the spreader that spread the fertilizer and lime to make the plants grow fast.

And it was Betty who pulled the cultivator down the rows to kill the weeds.

Johnny liked to work, too. He kept growing, and each year he got bigger. And each year he helped his father do more of the farm work. When Johnny was six he helped feed the hens and gather the eggs.

When he was nine he fed the pigs and the baby calves.

And when Johnny was twelve he helped his father milk the cows.

Every evening he climbed
up on Big Betty's broad back.
"Giddap, Betty!" he'd say
and they'd gallop
out to the pasture
to bring the cows
home to be milked.

Johnny made
Betty walk slowly
coming back
because he didn't
want the cows to get tired.

In the summer, when it was time to cut the hay for the cows to eat in the winter, it was Betty who pulled the mower that cut the grass.

And Betty who pulled the rake that raked it up.

And Betty who pulled home the big high loads of hay in the hay wagon.

Home to the big barn, where Johnny and his father piled up the hay in big, sweet-smelling mows.

When autumn came it was Big Betty who pulled home the wagonloads of corn and pumpkins, and the

wagonloads of red apples and beets and carrots, potatoes and cabbage to store in the root cellar.

There was work for Big Betty in the winter, too. The cows stayed in the barn all day and sleepily munched their hay. But Johnny and his father harnessed Betty and hitched her to the bobsled.

Then off they went to the woods to bring home wood for the big black stove in the farm kitchen. Johnny and his father sawed down the trees and sawed them up and split them and piled them up in the sled, and Betty hauled them home over the snow.

In the middle of the winter, when it was very, very cold, it was time to cut ice. Big Betty pulled the ice plow that marked off the square cakes on the big pond.

Johnny and his father sawed the ice and pulled the cakes out of the water and loaded them in the sled. Then Big Betty hauled them to the ice house.

There the ice was packed away in sawdust to keep until the hot summer, when it would be used in the milk cooler and in the farmhouse ice box.

When the first warm days of spring came and the snow began to melt, it was time to tap the maple trees. Johnny's father bored a hole in each tree and hung a bucket from

a spout to catch the sap. In the afternoons it was Big Betty who pulled the big tank on the sled from tree to tree while they gathered the sap. When the tank was full she pulled it to the sugarhouse, where it was boiled down into sweet maple sirup.

Every year as Johnny grew bigger Betty grew older. When Johnny was a big man Betty was an old horse, though she still felt strong and she still worked hard.

But one day Johnny said to his father, "Dad, poor old Betty's getting too old to do all the work on this farm. She gets tired when we plow the big field, and she can't walk fast enough when she pulls the mower."

And Johnny's father said, "Yes, I guess it's time we got a new young horse."

But even though Betty was old Johnny still loved her, and he didn't want to get a new young horse to take her place. He said, "I'd rather have a tractor, Dad."

Johnny's father thought it over. He knew how much work a tractor could do. More work than any horse. More work than any six horses, and the tractor would never get tired.

Then one day Johnny and his father went to the county fair. They looked at cows and chickens and pigs and sheep and horses and oxen.

And they looked at the big tractors, and then they bought one, a great big, new, shiny orange tractor with great big wheels.

And they bought a new plow for the tractor to pull, and a new harrow and a new planter and a new mower and a new rake and a big trailer to haul loads on.

Johnny took the big new tractor out to the big back field and plowed it all in half a day.

Big Betty looked over the fence and watched the tractor going round and round the field with the ground turning over behind it. She could hardly believe her eyes. It looked so easy and went so fast. She knew what hard work it had been for her, and she knew how many long days it had taken.

She wasn't surprised that Johnny was happy with the new tractor. But she wondered what would happen to her.

Johnny and his father decided to have an auction and sell the old plow and the old mower and all the old wagons that Betty used to pull. They put a notice in the paper and everybody

came to the auction. The auctioneer stood on a box and people bought the old wagons and the mower and the plow, while Betty looked out of her stall and watched.

Then, when everything had been sold,
the auctioneer said, "Well, now,
aren't you going to sell your horse?"

And then Big Betty felt very sad.
She didn't want to be sold and go to
a strange farm and leave her nice big
stall and her friends the cows.

But Johnny said to the auctioneer, "No, indeed!
We're not going to sell Betty. She's worked hard for us, and now if she's too old to work for us she's too old to work for any one else. We're just going to turn Betty out in the pasture and let her kick up her heels and eat grass and take it easy all the rest of her life."

When Betty heard that she knew she wasn't going to have to leave her home.

Then Johnny led Big Betty out of her stall and opened the pasture gate. And Betty galloped away and kicked up her heels because she was so happy.

Big Betty is still the one horse on the one horse farm. But she doesn't work any more. She just stands under the big shady trees in the meadow and watches the tractor doing all the work she used to do. And sometimes Johnny's little boy climbs up on her back and they go off in